ROCK RIVER

ROCK RIVER

BILL MAYNARD

G. P. PUTNAM'S SONS
NEW YORK

G. P. Putnam's Sons, Reg. U.S. Pat. & Tm. Off.
Published simultaneously in Canada. Printed in the United States of America.
Designed by Gunta Alexander. Text set in Simoncini Garamond

Library of Congress Cataloging-in-Publication Data
Maynard, Bill. Rock river / Bill Maynard. p.   cm.
Summary: Twelve-year-old Luke's summertime adventures along the
river are haunted by the memory of his older brother Robert, who
died being a daredevil in the same place a year and a half earlier.
[1. Rivers—Fiction. 2. Courage—Fiction. 3. Brothers—Fiction.
4. Death—Fiction.] I. Title. PZ7.M4675Ri   1998
[Fic]—DC21   97-42156 CIP AC
ISBN 0-399-23224-9   First Impression

For my editor, Susan Kochan, who believed in Ned and suggested Luke.

CONTENTS

1·THE ROCKS

Come on, Luke. You can make it," Ursula shouted over the roar of the rapids.

I looked at the river between us, and I wasn't too sure. The water ahead was dark and deep, and the currents were swift. I thought of the barbed wire that sometimes got dragged down from upriver farms by the winter ice and got hung up out of sight beneath the surface.

And I thought about Robert.

The rocks stretched from shore to shore as if some giant gravel truck had tipped over and spilled them across the river. Some had bumps that bruised your feet. Others were smooth and coated with damp, slimy moss. A few were enormous—the size of houses. Some of these big ones still had logs on top that had come crashing downstream when the water was high.

"Let's go, Luke," she called, cupping her hands to her mouth like a cheerleader. "I haven't got all day."

"Keep your pants on," I yelled back and then felt like a total idiot when I realized what I had said.

We had made it this far by leaping from rock to rock across the rapids. Ursula had gotten way ahead of me because I was being too careful as usual, and it was slowing me down. Ursula claimed that she had crossed the whole river once without ever touching the water. It was hard to imagine that anybody—especially a girl—could make it all the way dry, but Ursula was a great jumper and her legs were longer than mine. We were the same age, but she had gotten taller faster.

I finally caught up to her on Shipwreck Rock. Milo had named it because it looked like a three-decker ship that was sinking sideways into the water.

"Took you long enough," she complained. Her blond hair was hanging down in her eyes as she studied the next jump. It was a long one over a really fast current. The nearest rock was small, smooth, and wet with spray. As usual, she jumped first, flinging her long arms ahead of her, barely reaching the first rock with one foot and letting her weight carry her forward to a bigger, drier rock a couple of feet beyond.

Now it was my turn. I stared at the black moving water.

"What's the matter, Luke? Are you chicken?" she asked.

It was a good question. Was I brave or wasn't I? I spent a lot of time wondering about that. I didn't think I was a coward, but I knew what my mother would say if she saw me about to leap across more than four feet of swirling current hiding who-knows-what to a smooth slippery rock about the size of my Uncle Joe's bald head. "Don't take chances, Luke," she'd say. "You can't trust the river." And I knew she'd be remembering what happened to Robert.

Slowly, I turned away from Ursula and took the first of the many small jumps that would take me back to where we started. I knew she'd be disgusted with me. And I knew she would keep on going, taking incredible leap after leap until she ran out of rocks. Did I hear her laughing at me or was I just imagining it? Milo and Charlie were waiting on shore at the edge of the mudhole. They were watching Ursula.

"She's not human," Milo grumbled. "She's part kangaroo."

2 · THE BEACH

After I reached the shore, Milo, Charlie, and I took the path that curved around behind the mudhole. The weeds were so tall on each side that they shut out the sunlight, giving the place a dim, twilighty feel. The warm mud squished between our bare toes, and there was that great damp riverbank smell that always meant vacation and summer to me.

Milo led the way. I followed. Charlie tagged along in the rear. Milo's back looked like a map of the month of July. It was dark brown from the sun and covered with scratches and mosquito bites. He was thin and his shoulder blades stuck out like wings, but I knew he was strong. Milo and I were the same age—we'd both be twelve in the fall—but because I was more cautious, Milo usually went first. Sometimes I got tired of being so careful. Charlie was only eight, so he was lucky we let him come along at all. At least I'm braver than Charlie, I told myself. Milo and Charlie were brothers. I didn't have a brother anymore.

"Bees in the path. Bees overhead," warned Milo.

He sang it out like a lookout sighting trouble. Milo was usually pretending to be somebody else. Right now, he was probably a big game hunter on safari, leading our party through the thick African bush. But he was right about the bees. We had to watch where we stepped so that we wouldn't put a bare foot down on one of the wasps that were gathering the gooey mud for their nests. And there was a loud humming in our ears from other bees that were busy in the purple flowers above our heads. My grandmother called these riverbank flowers "rebel weeds," but I didn't know if that was still their name. Sometimes Grandma called things by names that nobody else used anymore.

Between you and me, I was never too fond of the mudhole path. It wasn't just the bees. You couldn't see far enough ahead to spot snakes. And nettles pushed in toward your bare skin from both sides. Charlie didn't like it, either. "I wish we were wearing more than our bathing suits," he said.

"We'll track the filthy pirates to their cave," Milo roared.

I wondered what new adventure was going on in his

head. But before I could find out, the path widened and brightened and we came out on the stretch of coarse sand and pebbles that we'd christened "the Beach."

Ursula's older sister, Hannah, was sitting there reading. She looked up and smiled. It was hard to believe that Hannah and Ursula were sisters. Ursula liked to fish and swim and jump rocks. Hannah always had her nose in a book.

"Let's go swimming," Charlie said, sneaking a look at Milo.

"Give me strength," muttered Milo, striking his forehead with the palm of his hand. "That's just exactly the kind of a *stupid, selfish, childish* thing I've learned to expect from you, Charlie." Here we go, I thought.

"What's wrong with swimming?" Charlie asked. He stared down at the sand.

"It doesn't *accomplish* anything," explained Milo, sounding annoyed. "It doesn't *discover* anything. It doesn't *capture* anything. *It doesn't catch any fish.*"

"But it's fun," protested Charlie. "And it makes you cool when you're hot. Right, Luke?" He turned to me for support.

I wanted to go swimming too, but not enough to get involved. I'd heard it all before. I just shook my head as if I couldn't be bothered to answer and wandered down to the edge of the river where I watched tiny minnows flash back and forth in the shallows.

This was the best place to swim in the river—the smoothest and safest. The current was weak, and after you swam out a few yards, the water was over your head. Best of all, there weren't any rocks to bash into. The rest of the river was wall-to-wall boulders—not just the ones you could see but also the ones that were out of sight. "Dumped here by a glacier," my father said. I didn't care how they got there, but I liked the way they broke up the river into the rapids and pools where smallmouth bass hung out.

Although we fished all over, we never swam anywhere but here. Except for my brother, of course. Robert would dive off practically any rock in the river. "Just dare me," he'd say. And then he'd do it. It used to scare me to watch. I was afraid he'd get hurt. He told me he knew where the underwater stuff was hidden, but there was no way that he could have remembered it all.

One time, back when I was only about Charlie's age, Robert dove into a shallow pool when the water was cloudy and just missed hitting a rock head-on. He scraped some skin off his chest and banged up one leg as he skidded over the sharp top of the rock. Mom yelled at him while she was putting first aid cream on his chest and sticking a big Band-Aid on his knee. Then she sent him to bed.

"Why?" she asked my father. "What makes him do it? What is he trying to prove?"

"He can't get As in school," Dad said. "So, he tries to get them on the river." I didn't figure out what Dad meant until I was older.

Standing there on the beach made me miss Robert more than ever, but my thoughts were interrupted by that sudden swishing sound that frightened minnows make when they scatter and fling themselves through the surface. Charlie was entering the water. He paused at the edge, then waded out a few feet to put some distance between him and Milo. "I know why you never want to go swimming," he muttered under his breath.

Milo heard him and gave him one of those "Watch yourself" looks that big brothers give kid brothers when they get out of line. "Swimming's a waste of time," Milo said. "And if we spend all our time floating around like a bunch of water lilies, *we're going to lose the bet.*"

Hannah smiled. "You're going to lose anyway," she said. "Nobody knows the river like Ursula."

That's for sure, I thought. Ursula and Hannah grew up on the river. They lived on their farm year round, an hour's bus ride from school. Milo and Charlie and I only came out from town for our summer vacations. The river wasn't that far from town, but it was a different world out here.

Charlie kicked water toward the beach, being careful not to get any on Milo. "We've got all summer to win the stupid bet," he said. I was surprised. He usually did whatever Milo told him. I sat down on the beach and waited to see what happened.

"All summer, Charlie? All summer?" asked Milo. His voice was getting higher, and his black hair stuck out straight at the sides like sticks in a hawk's nest. "This is the third week in August, Charlie. We'll be back in school in *two weeks!*"

"Oh, no," I groaned, covering my ears with my hands and rolling over backwards onto the sand with my feet up in the air. "Not the *S* word, Milo! I don't want to think about it."

"We *have* to think about it," Milo replied. "Because we have less than fourteen days left to preserve our honor as the Kings of the River." I could tell he was starting up another story in his head. "We must triumph over these natives, men!" he bellowed. "Or we'll have to spend the whole winter feeling like losers."

Hannah laughed. "You'd better get used to the feeling, Milo," she said. "You guys don't have a chance."

3·THE BET

I sure hoped that Hannah was wrong. I remembered the night that we made the bet.

We were having a cookout in back of the Perkins farmhouse. I could see Mr. Perkins, Ursula and Hannah's father, sitting in the kitchen in his undershirt reading the newspaper. He worked hard in his fields all day, and he liked to spend the evenings in his kitchen chair. It was a big farm that ran a good distance up and down this side of the river. My grandfather had built his summer cabin on a piece of the farm a long time ago. A few years later, Charlie and Milo's grandparents had added their cabin halfway between our place and the farmhouse.

After we'd gobbled the hot dogs and hamburgers, we

had started to tell ghost stories. Ursula was in the middle of a good one.

"So, you see, these fisherman—who really and truly lived *right around here* about a hundred years ago—were starving," she said. "So they snuck up on the old trapper as he slept in his cave and they murdered him."

"Why'd they do that?" Charlie wondered.

"So they could cut out his liver and use it for bait," Ursula said. Charlie looked sorry that he had asked. "And ever since then, on the darkest nights, when the mist rises up off the river, you're liable to see the old trapper walking along with his lantern and calling out, 'Who's got my liver? Who's got my liver? Who's got my liver?' "

The fire was burning low. It threw a dim, flickering light on our faces. Ursula got up and walked behind us. "Who's got my liver?" she repeated, softly. "Who's got my liver?"

"YOU'VE GOT IT!" she shouted when she was right behind Milo. The poor guy spilled his Coke all over his pants. I thought Charlie would never stop laughing.

After that, Ursula and Milo and I stuck some marshmallows on sharp sticks and held them close to the fire. I knelt in the smoke to keep away the mosquitoes. Hannah took out her book and tried to make out the words by the firelight. Charlie ran around with a glass jar, chasing lightning bugs in spite of Milo's sneers.

"Very brave, Charlie," Milo said. "The great hunter comes face to face with the ferocious lightning bug."

Then Milo's marshmallow burst into flame.

Ursula cracked up, watching Milo huffing and puffing, trying to put out the fire. In less than a minute there was nothing left but a black lump on the end of his stick. "Gosh, Milo," Ursula said. "Can't you do anything right?"

I felt sorry for Milo. He hated it when he did something dumb, and he would never admit that there was anything he couldn't do. Also, I think he really wanted the girls to like him. One time, Ursula and Hannah ranked the three of us to tell us who they liked best. They said that Charlie came first because he was the smallest and cutest and had curly hair. I finished second because I was good at a lot of things, but Ursula thought that I was a wimp on the rocks. They ranked Milo last because he was always pretending to be somebody else and he smelled like bait. You'd think Milo would have known they were kidding, but he disappeared for the rest of the day. When I finally found him, I could tell he'd been crying.

And I knew he was upset now by what Ursula had said. "I do *many* things right," he protested, shaking the black, gooey lump at her. "The fact is, I am an awesome explorer, a fearless leader of men, and the greatest fisherman to ever cast a line in this river."

"The greatest fisherman?" Ursula asked quietly, raising an eyebrow.

Uh-oh, I thought. Now Milo's in for it. Ursula and Hannah had both been fishing the river since practically before they could walk. They knew every smallmouth pool and bluegill nest as well as they knew their own names.

"The greatest fisherman, Milo?" Ursula repeated. "You'll have to prove it to me."

"No problem," Milo bragged. "Why, if I don't catch a bigger bass than either you or Hannah by the end of the summer . . ."

"You'll eat a night crawler," interrupted Ursula.

"Yuk!" said Hannah, looking up from her book.

Milo gulped as if he could already feel the slime in his mouth, but he couldn't back down now. "All right, I'll eat a night crawler," he said.

"It's a bet," Ursula said. "And Hannah and I are so sure that we'll win, you can use Luke and Charlie to help you. You can *all* eat night crawlers."

Oh, great, I thought. I always wanted to try a worm sandwich.

"And if *you* lose?" asked Milo.

"Impossible," said Ursula.

"Unthinkable," added Hannah.

"But if you do . . . ?" Milo persisted.

"You name it," Ursula said, defiantly.

"You'll both dye your hair green for the first day of school," Milo said.

4·THE BULL

Ow! Darn!" Charlie was really hurting. "We should have worn shoes, Luke."

He was right, of course, but I didn't answer. You could ruin your reputation by agreeing with somebody's kid brother.

Milo was wearing a pail like a helmet. Charlie was nibbling at our bread supply. The three of us were picking our way from grass patch to grass patch because the road had been covered with smashed rocks to keep it from getting muddy when it rained. It was like walking on spear points and arrow heads. Sometimes I felt like I spent my whole summer trying not to step on the wrong things.

"Is this trip necessary?" I asked, whacking my back with the net to discourage a horsefly.

"The best bait will get the biggest fish," Milo said, sounding like he was quoting from some fishing bible. "And we all know that the best bait is a fat, juicy shiner from Baitfish Brook."

"Which just happens to be on the other side of a hundred cows," Charlie said.

"More like a dozen," said Milo. "Grow up, Charlie. Cows won't hurt you."

"What about the bull?" I asked. My mother had warned me about the bull.

"He's in a different pasture," Milo said. "We won't even see him. Hey, look at that." He paused in the middle of the road.

"At what?" Charlie was busy staring down at road.

"Up there, in the hickory tree."

"If I look up, these stones will chop my feet into hamburger," Charlie said.

"A hornets' nest," Milo explained. "Wow. Look at the size of it."

Charlie and I stopped and stared up into the tree. It was hard to see because the sun was in our eyes, but about ten feet from the top I could make out a big gray sack hanging down from a branch. It looked like it was made out of wrinkled paper. There was a hole in the bottom. If I squinted I could see the hornets zipping in and out.

Milo put down his pail and picked up a flat piece of stone. He held out his left arm toward the nest. "The sniper adjusts his sights and draws a bead on the enemy outpost," he whispered.

"Forget it, Milo," I warned him.

"Well, if I scaled this between those two branches, I bet I could hit it," he said.

"If you were dumb enough," I said. "My grandmother says that if you throw something at a white-faced hornets' nest, they can travel right back down its path to whoever threw it. She says that getting stung by a hornet is like getting kicked by a mule. She knew somebody who got stung on the forehead once and was knocked out cold."

"And how fast could we run?" asked Charlie. "My feet are killing me."

Milo tossed the rock about a foot into the air and caught it. Then he did it again. He hated to give up on an adventure. Finally, he threw the rock toward the side of the road, pretending he had seen something in the bushes.

"We'll spare them for now, men," he said, switching into his platoon leader voice. "But their time will come. Right now we have bigger fish to fry."

"You mean to catch," Charlie said. I gave him a groan, and Milo faked a swing at him.

"Where are the cows?" I asked, when we reached the pasture.

"Maybe they're over behind that hill," Charlie suggested.

"A whole herd of cows behind one little hill?" Milo snorted. "Get real, Charlie. This pasture is totally empty. Old Man Perkins must have moved the cows somewhere else. Let's go."

A stone wall topped with barbed wire separated the pasture from the road. We climbed up on the wall and took turns holding the barbed wire apart, so that each of us could climb through without getting scratched. Then we started across the field, which slanted downhill like a ski slope from the road to the brook at the back. You could tell where the brook was because of the row of willow trees.

A deep gulley ran down the middle of the pasture almost all the way from the stone wall to the willows. At each end it was shallow, not much more than a ditch, but toward the middle the walls were high and steep. It looked sort of like a tunnel without a roof. Off to the right was the hill with a couple of scraggly trees on top.

We were walking along slowly, looking down at the ground to make sure we didn't plunk our bare feet into the smelly cow plops that were lying all over the place, when we heard a snort—not loud, not near, but absolutely, definitely, positively a *snort.* All three of us looked up at once. We watched a black bump appear on the top of the hill. The bump had horns.

"The bull," Charlie whispered.

"Quick! Into the gully!" Milo commanded. We went down on all fours and scrabbled along like giant crabs as fast as we could until we hit the edge of the ditch and threw ourselves over, tumbling down the steep bank into a heap at the bottom.

"I don't really like this," said Charlie.

"Let's get out of here *fast,*" I said.

"Without getting our bait?" Milo asked.

Charlie and I looked at each other. We couldn't believe what we had heard.

"Without getting our bait?" I said, imitating Milo. "Are you nuts, Milo? There's a bull out there. I don't feel like being a bullfighter today."

"Especially not today," said Charlie.

"Calm down, guys," Milo said. "The bull's way around behind the hill. He doesn't even know we're here. This gulley runs almost all the way to the brook. If we stay in the bottom, he'll never see us. Once we're in the water we'll be totally safe."

"Until it's time to go home," I said. "No way."

"If Robert were here, he'd do it," Milo said. Charlie looked away. I felt like Milo had punched me in the stomach. He had never come right out in the open and compared me to Robert before.

"Maybe that's why he's not here," I said. Now I felt *really* rotten. It was tough enough to have had an older brother who had been a superbrave daredevil. It was even worse after he got himself killed.

5·ROBERT

My brother, Robert, had been three years older than me, and I could never tell what he was going to do next. I remember one day when he got a report card that was even worse than usual. That evening, when Dad came home from work and was getting out of his car, he heard someone calling his name. He looked up, and there was Robert, sitting on the roof of the house.

"What are you *doing* up there, Robert?" Dad asked.

"Just trying to get my marks a little higher," Robert said.

If Dad thought it was funny, he didn't show it. First, he made Robert get down. Then he grounded him for a month. It wasn't because of his marks, Dad said. It was because of the dangerous things he did.

That night, Mom tried to explain to me why Robert had such problems in school. "You know how much you like to read, Luke?" she asked. I nodded. "Well, Robert sees the words all jumbled up and backwards," she said. "As if they were in a mirror. Sometimes he can't make any sense out of them. It makes it hard for him to study."

I tried to imagine what it would be like if I wasn't able to make any sense of the writing on the blackboard and I couldn't read my books anymore. No wonder Robert got upset and acted crazy. Maybe that's why he was always trying to prove he was superbrave.

Robert was as quick with numbers as he was slow with words. When he helped out in the store, Dad would have him add up the orders in his head to impress the customers. They'd be amazed at how fast he could give them the total. But words were a different story. Once he painted a sign for the window and some of the letters were backwards. A lot of people noticed. Some of them pointed and laughed. Robert wouldn't go back to the store for a week.

And then he was gone, and I didn't have a brother anymore. It happened early in the spring, about a year and a half ago. Dad's store was closed because it was Sunday. He and Robert and I had driven out from town to check the cabin for winter damage. Sometimes branches blew down and punched holes in the roof or raccoons got in and chewed things up. A bunch of Robert's friends had come along for the ride in the back of the pickup.

After we all piled out of the truck, Dad went to check on the cabin and the rest of us ran down to the river. Right away, Robert started to clown around. He was always ready to try something crazy. It was only April and the river was way out of control, still running high from the winter snows and pushing up over the banks in places. Robert began to walk a log between a high part of the land and the top of a big rock several yards offshore. His stupid friends kept egging him on.

I was looking away, so I don't know whether he slipped or lost his balance. There were other rocks just above the surface, so he could have hit his head when he fell. Or maybe the current was so fierce he couldn't make it to shore. I remember running along the bank, yelling and screaming until I couldn't see him anymore. Then I sat down and cried.

Mom had wanted to sell the cabin and never come back. Dad said that you couldn't run away from a place just because something bad happened. They acted as if it was their fault. You'd think they'd tried to walk the log instead of Robert. Dad kept trying to put it behind them, but Mom wouldn't let it go. She couldn't seem to think or talk about anything else. Finally, Dad couldn't take it. He stayed at work later and later. I guess he couldn't face coming home.

It made them fight about me. "You can't protect him from *everything*," Dad would say. But Mom had changed. Now she saw danger everywhere. "Well, he's all I've got left," she would answer. Then she'd start to cry and begin to go over it all again, and Dad would get angry and leave for the store. They hadn't agreed on much since Robert's accident. But I was pretty sure that neither one of them would want me to be sharing this pasture with a big black bull.

"Are you coming or not?" Milo asked, sounding impatient. I didn't want to speak to him after what he had said, so I just shook my head, turned around, and headed back toward the road.

It took me a while to get there, moving slow and staying low in the gulley so the bull couldn't see me. When I finally reached the wall, I climbed up on top of it. From there I could see Milo and Charlie, crouched over and sneaking along the bottom of the ravine toward the brook. And I could see the bull. He hadn't moved very much. I knew Charlie was scared, and he was only going along with this because of Milo. Milo was right about one thing: If Robert had been there, he would have been leading the way.

Was I being too cautious again? So far, the bull hadn't been able to see Milo and Charlie. He hadn't even noticed me when I climbed up on the wall. I could see a lot more of him from where I stood, and he was huge, a real bruiser. There was a bright flash and I figured it was probably the sunlight hitting the ring in his nose. Then he started to trot toward the gulley.

"Milo! Charlie!" I shouted. "Stay down! The bull!"

Milo and Charlie stopped and hunkered down lower. The walls on each side of them were straight as cliffs and about ten feet high. They stared up at the top of the bank. I tried to imagine how it looked to them when the bull stuck his head over the edge and Milo and Charlie got a good view of the slobber drooling down from his chin and the ring hanging out of his nose.

Luckily, the bull couldn't figure out how to get down to them. He just stood up above, snorting and pawing the ground, and shaking his big thick head from side to side. For a moment, it was a standoff. Then the bull started to move off toward the brook.

Oh, no, I thought. He's going for the low spot where he'll be able to walk right into the gulley down near the brook. Once he's in it, he'll come roaring back up it like a freight train. And Charlie and Milo will be right in front of him.

"Run for it, guys!" I yelled. "He's heading for the other end of the gully!"

Charlie and Milo leaped up and started toward me on a dead run. I saw the bait pail go flying. It looked real strange with Charlie and Milo in the bottom of the gulley heading in one direction and the bull on the high ground headed the opposite way, but I knew that wasn't going to last for long.

"Come on, guys. You can make it," I yelled. It was

uphill all the way, and I hated to think what the rocks and thistles were doing to their bare feet.

They were about fifty yards from the wall and and really sucking air when the bull made his turn and began to thunder up the ravine behind them. I could hear his hoofs hitting loose rocks and flinging them every which way. That plus the sound of his snorting gave Milo and Charlie a new burst of energy. I stood on top of the wall and held the two strands of barbed wire apart as far as I could.

Charlie and Milo were both yelling their heads off when they came up the last and steepest part of the hill. Charlie made the wall first, slipped between the strands of wire, and leaped down into the road. Milo got there a couple of seconds later, about ten feet ahead of the bull. He threw himself on the top of the stone wall and rolled under the barbed wire. He made it, but part of his bathing suit didn't.

The three of us crouched behind the wall, holding our breath and hoping that the bull didn't feel in the mood for high jumping today. After some snorting and pawing on the other side of the wall, we heard him amble back down the hill.

On the way home the sharp stones in the road were pure misery to what was left of Milo's and Charlie's feet. None of us was too happy, but Milo was miserable.

"What a bummer," he moaned. "No bait. No bait pail. No seat in my bathing suit."

He picked up a rock, and heaved it up through the tree limbs towards the round gray mass hanging down from a limb.

Grandma was right about white-faced hornets. Charlie didn't get stung at all. I only got stung once. But Milo got stung five times.

6 · GRANDMA

"Sometimes I wonder about that Milo," my mother said.

She gently patted a paste made from cornstarch and water all over the swollen part of my arm. Her long thin fingers felt smooth and cool against the simmering redness left behind by the hornet. We were standing near the old stone well outside our cabin. I had pumped out a bucket of water, and she was using it to wet the cornstarch.

"Milo's all right," I said. "He just gets carried away and does dumb things every now and then."

"That's what worries me," my mother said. She stared off into the distance. I wondered if she was thinking about Robert. I hated it when she got that look on her face. It always used to mean she was about to cry.

I walked to the edge of the yard and stared down at the river. The water rushing between the rocks made a special sound. I never got tired of it. My cot was outside, on the screened-in porch, and the roar of the rapids sang me to sleep every night. My mother hated the sound because she hated the river. If it weren't for Dad, she never would have let me go near it.

It hadn't always been like that. When I was little, she even went fishing with me and Robert. She was the only Mom I knew who could bait a hook. Not that she was all that keen on fishing. I think she just tagged along because she was afraid that Robert might talk me into doing something foolish.

She needn't have worried. Robert's specialty was "saving my life." If something was the least bit scary, he wouldn't even let me try. I was the family "scholar." *He* was the daredevil. And that was that. He always helped me before I needed help. One time when we were crossing some rapids he actually reached out and took my hand. The other kids saw it, and I felt like a jerk.

Then, Robert got killed, and Mom took over. She spent all her time worrying, telling me to watch out for this, be careful about that. It seemed like the whole world was one big danger. "Remember what happened to Robert," she'd say. How could I forget? No wonder I didn't know if I was brave or not. I'd never had a chance to find out.

The screen door slammed behind my grandmother as

she came out of the kitchen and into the yard. Grandma was as short and round as my mother was tall and thin. She had tiny tight white curls all over her head. Grandpa had built the cabin for Grandma because she'd been raised on a farm, and although she never complained about living in town, she liked to get away from close neighbors now and then.

I heard her chuckling and mumbling as she stepped down to the grass.

"She's talking to Grandpa," I whispered to my mother.

"Well, they always did everything together," Mom explained. "I guess they still do."

Grandma crossed to the well. She was wearing a long dress covered with big red flowers. She always looked dressed for church even when she was only taking a walk to the beach. Mom had changed, too, because it was almost time for Dad to come home. She had fixed up her hair, but the cornstarch on her hands made her look like she was still in the middle of baking a pie. I hoped that Dad wouldn't be late again.

"Well," Grandma said, putting her hands on her hips and spreading her elbows wide. "What have we here?"

"Luke got stung by a hornet," my mother explained.

"Murder!" said Grandma. She always said "murder" when something upset her. Nobody knew why. "Let me see that," she said.

I held out my arm.

"You're lucky, Luke. I knew someone who was stung by a hornet on the forehead once, and . . ."

"I bet he passed out," I interrupted. My mother shot me a look that said I was right on the edge of being fresh.

"Why, yes. As a matter of fact he did," Grandma said. She looked disappointed because her story had ended before it started. "Does it hurt awfully?"

"Feels just like I've been kicked by a mule," I replied. My mother shook her head and looked away, trying to hide her smile.

"Where did you run into hornets?" Grandma asked.

"On our way back from the cow pasture," I replied.

"What in the world were you doing there?" asked my mother. She had that worried look again.

"We were trying to get bait," I said. "We're going fishing tomorrow." I was hoping I could change the subject before I had to mention the bull.

"Well, you've had a bad day," Grandma said, not knowing the half of it. "After you eat your supper, you had better turn in early with one of your books."

"I can't, Grandma," I said. "We didn't get any baitfish, so we're going hunting for night crawlers tonight."

7 · THE LIGHTS

I can't see," Charlie complained.

"Tough," said Milo. "I told you to bring your own flashlight."

"I'd like to *see* them before I *feel* them," Charlie said. "What happens if I step on one in the dark?"

"First it'll squoosh," I said. "Then it'll slither out between your toes and slide back into its hole."

"No way!" Charlie said, as if he could prevent it just by saying it. "That does it," he muttered to himself. "I've got to start wearing shoes."

The night was pitch black with no moon. A thick mist was rolling up from the river. It made me think of the fog in those old black-and-white horror movies like *Jack the Ripper* and *The Hound of the Baskervilles.* Behind us some bats were jigging up and down by the bare bulb of the cabin's outdoor light, catching moths and other strange things in the air. The windows were dark because my father hadn't come home yet and my mother and grandmother were down at the Perkinses watching TV. It was only August, but it seemed like Halloween. I kept feeling spider webs brushing across my face, but maybe it was just the wet mist.

We were crouched down, moving along slowly, searching the far end of the lawn where the grass had been mowed, near the edge of the woods that ran down the side of the yard all the way to the cabin. Milo and I were side by side, out in front. Charlie was slipping and sliding along behind. The grass was soaked. We had hosed it down good before dark. It was either that or wait for rain to bring out the night crawlers. I was carrying a coffee can that was half full of dirt. We had punched air holes in its plastic lid.

An owl hooted once, then again.

"What was that?" Charlie asked.

"A giant, flying, gooey night crawler about to wrap itself around your scrawny neck," Milo said.

"Cut it out, Milo," Charlie said.

"Maybe it's the old trapper, looking for his liver," I said.

Nobody laughed.

"Who's got my liver?" I moaned, turning on my flashlight and holding it up like a lantern.

"Very funny," said Milo, sarcastically.

"Milo doesn't like ghosts," Charlie whispered to me. I thought he was kidding. Milo was usually so busy being somebody else that he never seemed scared. Maybe ghosts were an exception. He had such a good imagination, he could probably see things when they weren't even there.

"Shhh," Milo interrupted. "I see one."

"A ghost?" Charlie squeaked.

"A night crawler, stupid."

He eased the beam of his flashlight along the ground until we could just make out the long fat worm stretched out full length on the wet grass. Holding the flashlight in his left hand, Milo reached out slowly toward the worm with his right, but when his fingers were just inches away, it slid across the grass and disappeared in a hole. It looked like it had been sucked down like a strand of spaghetti.

"You touched it with the light," I said. "You have to shine the light *near* it, so it can't feel it."

"You can't *feel* light," Milo said.

"Oh, no?" I said. "Then what scared it back into its hole?"

"It heard Charlie blabbing," Milo said. "If you're such an expert, you try it." He still sounded mad.

I moved my flashlight beam slowly from side to side in front of me so that it wouldn't make any place bright for too long. A couple of mosquitoes hummed in my ears, but I couldn't risk the sound of a slap. It wasn't long before I spotted two more night crawlers, lying next to each other, almost touching.

"Freeze," I whispered, and all three of us turned into statues.

I pointed the light a couple of feet off to the side of the worms so that they were almost in darkness and I could just barely see them. I eased out my hand and grabbed one and held on tight but not too tight. He was only half out of his hole, and I didn't want to crush him as he tried to pull away. He felt cool and slimy. The other one zipped back into the ground.

"Don't yank. It'll break," Milo said, softly.

"I know that," I hissed.

Tugging slowly and steadily, I eased the worm out of the hole. Milo held out the coffee can. I dropped in the worm and Milo snapped on the lid.

"Well done, men," Milo said. "I'm proud of you." He had recovered and wanted to be in charge again.

That's when Charlie saw the light in the woods. "Look!" he said, pointing. "Someone's coming."

"Or some*thing,*" Milo said.

Whatever it was, it was still pretty far away and the mist made it hard to see. There was definitely some kind of light, but it looked fuzzy and out of focus because of the moisture in the air. The rays shot out in all directions the way a streetlight looks when you squint your eyes.

"He must have come up the path from the river," I said.

"*Who* must have?" Charlie asked.

"Whatever," I replied.

"It's flickering and swinging," Charlie said. "Do you think it's a *lantern?*" I knew he was remembering Ursula's story, but he didn't want to mention the old trapper.

"What do you think it is, Milo?" I whispered.

Milo didn't answer. I turned and shined the flashlight around behind me. It didn't help me see much because of the mist. But one thing was sure—*Milo was gone.* I couldn't believe it. I was pretty sure that if something had grabbed him, I would have heard it. And even if he were afraid of ghosts, I didn't think that Milo would run away. Maybe he was trying to sneak up on the light and get around behind it.

"Look! It went out," Charlie reported. He was still staring straight ahead toward the woods. "Wait a minute. Now there's another one, coming up the hill."

"Maybe it just moved," I said.

"It couldn't have," Charlie said. "They're too far apart. Could there have been *two* old trappers?" he whispered. He was only half kidding.

"Maybe they were brothers," I said.

"Can you see both of them, Milo?" he asked, turning around from the woods. "Milo?"

"Milo's missing," I said.

"Missing?" he hissed. "What do you mean 'missing'?"

"I can't find him," I said. "He seems to have disappeared."

"Milo!" Charlie called, whispering as loud as he

dared. He sounded angry and frightened at the same time. "Stop fooling around, Milo! I'm scared enough."

"Look, the second light's moving along the edge of the woods toward the cabin," I said. "And there's the first one again. They're coming together."

"Let's make a run for it," Charlie said.

"Hold on," I said. "We can't just run home and lock the doors and hide under the bed. Maybe somebody's lost. Or hurt. Down on the river. Maybe somebody needs help or something. We've got to find out."

"*You* find out," Charlie said. "I liked the part about locking the doors."

"Come on," I said, pointing the flashlight ahead of me and starting toward the woods. My mouth was dry and I was sort of scared, but I felt like I could handle it.

"Go toward them? No way!" Charlie said.

"Then stay here alone in the dark," I told him.

"Alone? In the dark? No way!" he said and he came stumbling along behind me.

As we got closer I could make out the lights bobbing along together just inside the edge of the woods. On. Off. On. Off. Both lights were blinking. Or maybe it was just the bushes in front of us, swaying in the breeze, that were blocking and then unblocking what we saw. Another owl hooted. There was a faint smell of skunk. Not now, I thought. That's all we need.

"Aren't you scared, Luke?" Charlie asked from behind me.

"Not scared enough to run," I said. At least I didn't think I was. It seemed like a good time to find out. As far as I knew, nobody ever got drowned while they were chasing ghosts in the woods.

When we were about twenty feet from the first row of trees, the lights disappeared. Charlie and I stopped and stood totally still, straining our eyes and our ears to try to make out whatever was out there in front of us.

"Hey!" I called. "In the woods. Anybody there? Come on out."

Nothing. Not a word. Not a sound but the soft sighing of the wind in the hemlocks and the steady chatter of the rapids below. Charlie and I waited, barely breathing. He was pushing up against me. I could feel by his trembling that he was just about ready to cut and run. Then a couple of stones rattled down the hill and we heard footsteps scrunching toward us.

"I'd rather not be here," Charlie whispered.

"Shhh," I said. "Just clam up and watch."

The bushes trembled, then parted and two figures—one slightly taller and slimmer than the other—stepped out of the woods and onto the edge of the field. When they turned on their lanterns, the flickering light on their faces made strange shadows that hid their eyes.

"Evening, boys," said Hannah with a ghastly grin.

"What's in the coffee can?" asked Ursula. "Your dinner?"

8 · THE KEEPER

They were *trying* to scare us," Charlie said the next day. "They did it on purpose."

"Maybe not," I said. "Ursula told me they'd gone down to see if the river was rising."

"After dark, carrying two old lanterns?" Milo stripped some line off his reel. "Believe that and you'll believe in the tooth fairy."

We were fishing from three different rocks. Each rock split the water into two separate currents. I watched my line. Whenever it straightened out on top of the water, I lifted it, swung the worm back, and dropped it next to my rock again. Fish were supposed to hang out in the deep water behind the rocks and wait for food to wash by.

"You sure disappeared in a hurry last night," I said to Milo, not taking my eyes off my line.

"He went home for another coffee can. Right, Milo?" Charlie said. "In case we caught a lot more worms."

Milo swung his bait to the top of the current. "I got bored. I knew it was Hannah and Ursula right from the start."

No way, I thought, but I kept my mouth shut. Why rub it in? I was busy wondering what had kept *me* there. Charlie had been shaking. Milo had run away. But good old Luke had stuck it out. Why? Maybe because I didn't hear any voices warning me to steer clear of ghosts. Maybe it takes real rocks and rapids to scare my mom and turn me into a wimp.

I could tell that Milo didn't want to talk about last night. He made a disgusted face. "The way these fish are biting, these worms will last us a hundred years," he said.

Charlie started to reel in his line. "Ursula says small-mouth bass are too proud to eat worms. She says that worms are for catfish and carp."

It wasn't *what* she said, it was *how* she had said it. "Might as well have those worms with warm milk for a bedtime snack," she had told us last night. "No self-respecting smallmouth is going to let himself to be caught on a night crawler."

"She talks too much," Milo said. "She thinks she knows everything."

"She knows the river," I replied. Ursula wasn't so bad.

She couldn't help it if she had grown up here. She kidded us a lot, but that was because she could do everything without hardly trying. She didn't have to show off. One time she and Robert tried to make the same jump. It was a long one, and you couldn't get much of a start. He was bigger and older, of course, but she made it dry, and he fell in and got drenched. He didn't like that at all. She wasn't trying to make him look bad, but he took it that way.

Charlie started to reel in his line. "Maybe we should go get some grasshoppers," he said.

"Too hot to float grasshoppers," said Milo. "The fish are deep. They won't come up in the daytime for anything on the surface."

"We could go swimming," Charlie said. He didn't sound too hopeful. When Milo scowled, he pretended to be untangling a backlash.

"Well, look who's here," I said.

Ursula and Hannah were picking their way out from shore about fifty yards below us. They were wading across the rapids to the small island of rocks just above the swimming hole. Ursula carried two fishing poles over her head. She was two years younger than Hannah, but she was taller. Hannah followed with a bucket and a blue coffee can.

"Should I tell them that the fish aren't biting?" I asked.

"After what they did last night?" asked Milo. "No way. Let them find out for themselves."

We watched as they stripped out some line and baited their hooks. We couldn't see what they took out of the can. Before long we had our own problems and we forgot the girls. My hook was snagged on the bottom. Milo had a snarl in his line. Charlie had given up completely and was just dangling his feet in the water.

That's when we heard two terrible words that made our blood run cold.

"Got one!" yelled Hannah. In spite of the distance and the noise of the rapids I heard her as clear as a bell.

"Oh, no," Charlie said. "I can practically taste those night crawlers."

The three of us watched Hannah play her fish. I knew it was no record setter because she was horsing it in pretty fast. But at least it was a fish, which was a lot more than we had to show for our morning of drowning worms.

"I don't believe it," Milo said. "Of all the rotten luck."

Then Hannah held up the fish, first to Ursula and then to us. She looked disappointed. We could see that it was undersized. Bass have to be ten inches or more to be "keepers." She unhooked it, moved it gently back and forth in the water, and let it go.

"Hah! Too small!" said Milo. But his relief didn't last long.

"Got one!" yelled Ursula, and began to reel in her line.

I could tell right away that this one was bigger. Ursula's rod tip was bent over, and Hannah was filling the bucket with water. It took Ursula three or four minutes to land it. When she finally lifted it out of the water, Hannah helped her measure it against the markings on her pole. Ursula smiled as she slipped the hook out and dropped the fish in their bucket. She turned toward us and held both hands over her head, spreading her fingers wide. Then she closed them and held up one finger.

"Eleven inches," I said. "That could win it."

"We have to find out what they're using for bait," Charlie said.

"Well, you wanted to go swimming," said Milo. "Go see what's in the can."

"They'll never show me."

"Then don't ask. Sneak up on them."

"Why me?"

"Because you're the smallest and the sneakiest, obviously."

"I'll go with you, Charlie," I said. "But we'll have to stay out of sight or we'll never get away with it."

Charlie and I slid down our rocks and eased into the river. It felt as cold as spring water because of the current and the fact that we had been sitting for hours in the sun. It felt good.

"The frog men leave the mother ship and paddle quietly toward the enemy gunboat," Milo said. There he goes again, I thought. I noticed that he wasn't doing the swimming. He was staying with the mother rock.

In the beginning the water was up to our necks. Then,

pretty soon, it was over our heads. We let the current carry us across the deep part of the pool. On the other side, when the water began to get shallow, we had to crouch and use both our hands and feet to slip and slide along. We were trying to keep the big rocks between us and the girls. In some places it got so shallow that we had to stretch out flat and bob along just using our hands on the bottom.

There was one really deep spot just upstream from the island. Charlie and I covered most of it under water. When we surfaced, we paddled along like a couple of bullfrogs with just our eyes and the tops of our heads above the water. I could see the blue coffee can at the back edge of the island on a flat rock about ten feet behind the girls. We eased up behind a tall flat rock that looked like a surfboard standing on end.

"You slip in and grab the can," I said. "Then you pass it to me." Because Charlie was smaller and thinner, he could slide through the shallows like a lizard, with his chin and his chest practically scraping the bottom. When he got close enough, he reached just his arm out of the water and closed his fingers around the can. It would have been "mission accomplished" if he hadn't scraped the bottom of the can on the rock, making a noise that sounded louder than a snow shovel scraping a sidewalk on a Sunday morning.

"Hey!" said Ursula as she spun around and saw us lurking in the shallows. "Where'd you guys come from?

Give me that!" She dropped her pole and charged across the island.

Frantically, I pried the lid off the can and looked inside.

"Hellgrammites!" I said. "No wonder. They're using hellgrammites. I knew they had better bait than us."

9 · HELLGRAMMITES

There are two ways to catch hellgrammites. Neither one is particularly enjoyable.

Hannah read that hellgrammites are dobsonfly larva, whatever that means. All I know is they live on their backs in our river, where they cling to the bottoms of the smaller stones. Whenever anybody says "rock bottom," meaning "the worst," it makes me think of hellgrammites.

Hellgrammites are not pretty. They have hard shell-like collars—the only safe place to grab them—and equally hard heads that end in curved double pincers with sawtooth edges. Both the heads and the collars are as black as a black widow spider, but shiny. When you put a hook in a hellgrammite, even the blood, or whatever it is that comes out, comes out black. Their bodies are grayish and have a tough, spongy feel as if they were made out of old rubber bands. Each body is surprisingly strong and can grab onto almost anything because it has plenty of legs on both sides plus a pair of hooks at the end.

Hellgrammites look like they come from outer space or maybe the dinosaur age. Like I said, they are ugh-ugh-ugly. They don't smell very good, either, and they can pinch hard enough to draw blood. Unfortunately, there are times when a smallmouth bass won't bite on anything else.

"Should we try the screen first?" Charlie asked.

He was carrying a piece of old window screen about two feet wide. We'd nailed narrow boards to the two opposite edges. The safest way to catch hellgrammites is to stick a screen upright in the water at the downstream end of some shallow rapids. You keep the water from pushing it over by holding the ends of the side sticks and bracing the screen against your knees. Somebody else turns over rocks upstream so the current can knock loose whatever is hanging on. If you're lucky, the screen is soon covered with hellgrammites, which you can pick off by their collars. At least that's the idea.

It doesn't always work that way. Sometimes you can turn over half the rocks in the river and nothing comes loose. Other times you'll see a big, fat hellgrammite twisting and turning in the current, but it will sweep right by to the right or the left. Now and then one will miss the screen and grab onto something else. That's why we like to keep the screen in front of our bare legs.

Charlie was holding the screen while Milo and I turned over rocks. After almost an hour of moving the screen and prying up stones, we only had three small hellgrammites in our coffee can. If we started fishing and one of us lost his bait, he would have to quit for the rest of the day or go back to worms.

"I guess we'll have to try it by hand," Milo said. I was afraid he was going to say that.

The other way to catch hellgrammites is by *feel*.

We left the screen on the beach and wandered down the edge of the river until we came to a stretch of slow water about two feet deep where the bottom was starting to get mucky. Round stones the size of small pillows lay scattered beneath the water.

The procedure is to pull up one side of a stone and slide your hand under. Then you feel all around on the bottom of the rock. When your fingers touch something rubbery, and you're pretty sure it's the body of a hellgrammite, you work your way up to its hard collar, grab it, and pull the hellgrammite free from the rock.

"What if I touch its head first?" Charlie didn't seem to eager to start.

Milo snorted. "Then you won't have to grab it."

"Why?"

"Because it'll grab you!"

Milo bent over and put both his arms in the water. He had an expression on his face like a surgeon in the middle of an operation. We couldn't see what he was doing because the minute he pried up a stone the water would cloud up with muck.

"And *that* is how it's done," he announced suddenly, straightening up and holding out a fat hellgrammite by its collar. Its body curled back and forth as it tried to grab onto his hand with the hooks on its tail.

"What if something else is under the rock?" Charlie asked. That part that worried me, too. I'd seen the black snakes that swam in this river. I didn't know if they lived under rocks, and I didn't want to find out.

"Are you telling me that Ursula and Hannah can do something that my own brother can't?" Milo asked.

Charlie sighed and bent over and started to feel around on the bottom. The water clouded as he lifted a rock.

"Yikes!" he shouted, straightening up and falling over backwards with a tremendous splash.

Out of the corner of my eye I saw a baby catfish, about three inches long, scoot out of the cloudy water and wiggle off.

"It was smooth and awful," Charlie said, shuddering. He was sitting up to his waist in the water. "And it twitched when I touched it."

"It was only a baby catfish," I said.

"A baby catfish?"

"I saw it swimming away."

Charlie seemed half relieved and half disappointed. "Well, it felt awful. And catfish can sting, you know. Anyway, it's your turn, Luke. You put your hand under one of these rocks and see how it feels."

I waded down the river a bit. Then I saw a rock that looked like a perfect upside-down house for a hellgrammite. I lifted one side and started to ease my hand underneath. I felt as if I was putting my hand into the mouth of a cave, and I didn't know whether the bear was home or not. I held my breath and I closed my eyes.

The bottom of the rock felt slimy as I slid my hand across. I felt my fingers touch something thick and rubbery. Then, almost immediately, I felt the same thing, about two inches away. A double! This would shut Milo up for a while.

I kept the rock tipped up with my knee while I leaned over and slid a hand in from each side. I was bent so low that my chin and chest were touching the water. Carefully, I felt my way up each hellgrammite's body to its hard collar and pulled it loose.

"Ta dah!" I cried, straightening up, and holding out the two hellgrammites.

Nobody was watching. Milo and Charlie were standing together a few feet away. They were staring out across the water. Milo had an angry look on his face.

"What's a stranger with a fishing pole doing on *our* river?" he asked.

10 · THE INTRUDER

Ursula whistled softly. "He must have spent a year's pay for that outfit."

Charlie and Milo and I had climbed up the bank for a better look. Ursula and Hannah had come down from the farmhouse to join us.

"Look at that vest and that fancy wicker creel," Milo said. "He's a walking Orvis catalog."

The fisherman had come onto the river from the far side. We could see his car, parked in the grove of trees just off the paved road. Right now he was below and directly in front of us and not too far away. His vest was bristling with flaps for its dozens of different sized pockets. His hat was pure Indiana Jones except for its wreath of fancy flies. There was a box on his belt to carry even more flies and a net hanging down at his side. We watched him move slowly across the river in his chest-high waders, shooting his line into the deeper pools. He seemed to be working his way toward the rocks above our swimming hole.

"He knows how to cast," Hannah said.

"Big deal," Charlie said. "Who needs to cast with currents like these?"

We watched the stranger false cast a few times to get a good length of line out. Then suddenly he shot it all forward in a graceful, rolling loop that dropped his fly gently into one of the pools. Hannah was right. He not only had the equipment. It looked like he knew how to use it.

"If this guy is good and he's lucky, he could take home the winner that one of us wants to catch tomorrow," I said.

"We can't let that happen," Ursula said. "This is *our* river." I was glad that she had included Milo and Charlie and me as part owners.

"What we need is a plan," Milo said.

If the fisherman was heading for our swimming hole, we didn't have much time. We marched single file down the path to hold a war council at the back of the beach. Once we got there, Milo and Ursula started pacing back and forth across the sand, each wanting to be the one who came up with the plan. The rest of us sat in a half circle, straining our brains.

Finally, Charlie broke the silence. "We could sneak out and hook his line to a log," he said.

"Are my eyes going bad, Charlie?" Milo asked. "I don't seem to see any scuba gear lying around."

Charlie waited a minute, then he tried again. "We could lead him to a deep spot so his waders would fill up."

There were groans all around. "Take a nap," Ursula said.

Then, suddenly, Milo clapped his hands together. "Here's the strategy, troops," he said. "When he gets here, we'll hide in the bushes and bomb the pool with boulders."

"Until he complains to our parents, and we all get grounded for the rest of the summer," Hannah said. "Honestly, Milo. You seem to think you can solve all the world's problems by throwing rocks."

Tell me about it, I thought, rubbing my arm.

"We could bang some stones together *under* the surface," Ursula said, "because sound is louder and travels better under water."

Nobody said anything, but Milo made a big show of holding his nose. Ursula stuck out her tongue at him.

"I think we're going about it wrong," I said. All the heads turned toward me. I gulped and went on: "You're all trying to scare the fish. Maybe we should scare the fisherman."

It was quiet for a minute. Then Ursula spoke. "Sounds good to me," she said. "How do we do it, Luke?"

She walked over and sat down. Milo waited a second

and then reluctantly joined her. I stood up, brushed the sand off the seat of my bathing suit, and walked to the middle of the beach. My heart was thumping. I was trying to think fast. I wondered what Robert would have thought if he could have seen me.

"Come on, Luke. Lay it on us," Hannah said.

I took a big breath and started. "What we have to do is convince this guy that this is the worst place in the world for him to be," I said. "We have to make him think he ought to get out of here as fast as he can and never come back."

Milo groaned. "And that's your idea?"

"Give him a chance," Ursula said. "Go ahead, Luke. How do we convince him?"

"We'll divide it up," I said. A plan was beginning to take shape in my head. "We'll tell some whoppers," I continued.

"Like what?" Milo was getting interested. He loved to make things up.

"Whatever it takes," I said. "Milo, your job is to get him to believe that he's wasting his time here, that he won't catch anything but a cold, that all the good fish have been dead and gone for years."

Milo rolled up his eyes. "That's it?" he said. "Shouldn't be too difficult with the luck we've been having."

"Hannah," I went on, ignoring the face that Milo was making. "You make him worry about the water. Make him think that this pool is so rotten and polluted that it will eat the waders right off his feet."

"And smell up his fancy new vest," Ursula added.

"And you, Charlie, you've got to scare him out of his skin," I said. "You've got to make him believe that this part of the river is dangerous, that something really bad will happen to him if he stays here."

"Hey, this is fun," Charlie said.

"What about me, Luke?" Ursula asked. "What's my part?"

"You've got the toughest job. You have to get him to leave *right away*. You've got to get him out of here before he catches anything."

Ursula half-closed her eyes and tipped back her head. It looked like she was squinting to keep the sun out of her eyes. We all waited. When she started to smile, I knew that she was getting an idea. Finally, she opened her eyes.

"I'll send him upriver," she said.

"Upriver! For what?" Milo said. "There's nothing decent up there. Only crummy catfish and muddy old carp. Nobody ever fishes in that part of the river."

"He doesn't know that," Ursula said.

"What makes you think he'll believe there are bass up there?" Charlie asked.

"Because I'll make it sound like we're trying real hard to keep him from finding out," Ursula replied.

Even I had to smile. It was complicated, but it might

work. I crossed the beach, then turned and paused at the entrance to the path that ran behind the mudhole. "Does everybody know what to do?" I asked.

Milo struck his Winston Churchill pose and held up two fingers in a V for victory. "Men," he said. "And women," he added, bowing to Hannah and Ursula. *"This* will be our finest hour."

11·SNAKE ISLAND

The water between the shore and the island was swift and shallow. At first it was only up to our knees, but soon it pushed higher against the tops of our legs and soaked the bottoms of our bathing suits. Milo was leading the way. Charlie came last, clutching our precious cargo of hellgrammites as if he was afraid that they might escape or be stolen if he didn't carry them with him.

The fisherman had arrived at the island already. At first he was too busy with his casting to see us or hear us. Over and over he flipped his wet fly across the current on the other side of the island and worked it back toward him as it swung into the quiet water below.

Milo was the first one to climb out, dripping water all

over his rock. The rest of us were strung out across the rapids behind him.

The fisherman started another cast, but when he turned to watch his line stretch out behind him, he caught sight of our parade from the corner of his eye. "What the . . ." he sputtered. "Am I being invaded?"

Nobody answered. One by one we splashed out of the water and took up positions on the rocks around him. He took a step toward the far side of the island. "It's a free river, kids," he said. "But there's not much room here. Isn't this going to be kind of crowded?"

"Especially when the snakes come out," Charlie said.

"Snakes?"

"You're on Snake Island, mister," Charlie said. "When the sun warms things up, there will be a dozen big black snakes stretched out on every single one of these rocks."

Letting his line drift for a minute, the fisherman climbed to a higher stone. He bent over and tried to look under the rocks that were closest to his feet. Whether he believed Charlie or not, he wasn't taking any chances. "I'm not too fond of snakes," he said.

"Neither are we. They ate the fish," Milo said.

"No fish?" the fisherman asked.

"Not here," Milo added. "This part of the river was fished out long ago."

"The snakes got what was left," Charlie explained.

"Except for what had already died," Hannah said.

"Died?" asked the fisherman. He had on a bewildered expression, but I still couldn't tell how much of this stuff he was swallowing.

"Because of the water," Hannah said. "Even if you caught a fish you couldn't eat it."

"What's wrong with the water?"

"It's full of those letters," Charlie piped up.

"Letters?"

"He means PCBs," I said. "But there are worse things than that. Toxic chemicals and sewage. Nasty stuff." I sounded like Miss Hasbrouck teaching environment in fifth grade.

"And those flies are worthless," said Milo, pointing to the bright bits of fluff and feathers on the fisherman's hat. "The fish in this river won't take artificials."

"Well, that's all I've got."

"They're no good in this water," Milo said. "It's too full of junk."

"What kind of junk?" the fisherman asked.

"That kind of junk," I said, pointing to a cedar shingle, a milk carton, and two grapefruit skins that were circling slowly in the still water behind a tangle of brush. "Whatever's not nailed down when the river rises ends up in the water."

"And I suppose the river gets really high," said the fisherman, smiling.

"See those?" I asked, pointing at a couple of logs that were balanced on two of the highest rocks. "You get a good cloudburst, and this island will be under six feet of river before you can reel in your line."

"Not the best place to fish it seems," the fisherman said, still smiling. Did he believe us or had we overdone it? "Snakes and pollution," he continued. "Floods. And no fish. Maybe I should consider trying my luck somewhere else."

We tried not to look happy.

"Any suggestions?" he asked, looking around at all of us.

"Downstream's the best," Ursula said. "For the big ones, I mean. They catch sixteen inchers down there," she added.

"Sixteen inches," the fisherman said. "That's a mighty big smallmouth. But are you sure you mean *down*stream? Doesn't the river widen out down there and get shallow? I've heard there are wall-to-wall weeds."

"Maybe that's where the big ones hide," Charlie volunteered. Milo gave him a look.

The fisherman stared hard at Charlie. Then he turned back to Ursula. He looked like he had just figured something out. "Where's the *worst* place to fish in your river?" he asked her with a very serious expression.

Ursula pretended to be thinking. "Well, of course, upriver is completely worthless," she said. "You'd never want to go there. It's slow and muddy. About a mile from here there's a farmer who keeps some boats for the summer boarders to row around. But nobody would fish there." At least that's the truth, I thought.

"No bass at all? You're sure about that." He was getting excited.

"No *fish* at all," Charlie said.

"Except maybe a catfish or two," Milo said quickly. "Or maybe a dumb old carp."

"And, of course, you wouldn't recommend that I go there?" He was starting to reel in his line.

"You'd be totally wasting your time," Ursula said.

"Well, I guess downstream it is," he said. "I'll have to go back to my car." He took off his hat and examined the flies that were stuck in his hatband. "But you say these won't work. I'd need live bait. Didn't I see you boys catching hellgrammites when I first came out on the river? I'll pay a dollar apiece."

"They're awful hard to find," Milo said.

"And dangerous," Charlie said, clutching the can to his chest.

"Well, it's up to you," said the fisherman. "You kids seem to think I'll do better downstream, but I'd have to have bait."

"You can have these," I said, taking the can from Charlie. "We won't be needing them anymore."

12 · THE LEANING TREE

Did you have to give him our bait?" Milo asked. Being a leader wasn't all glory. My decision to give up the hellgrammites was getting mixed reviews.

"He wouldn't have left without it," I said.

"I bet my snake story helped," Charlie said with a grin.

After the fisherman left the island, I had suggested that we keep an eye on him to make sure that he didn't sneak back to our fishing hole. Charlie and Milo and I were trailing him from our side of the river, moving as fast as we could along the narrow path that led upstream from the beach. Ursula and Hannah had gone home to help their father pick beans.

"Do you think he fell for it?" Milo asked.

"We'll know in a minute," I said.

The path hadn't been used much and was overgrown with saplings. Milo went first, pushing the branches aside with his hands. I had to be careful that they didn't snap back into my face when he let go. Charlie was getting the same treatment from me.

"I hate being last," Charlie muttered.

"He was heading for his car when we started out," Milo said. "But I can't see him anymore."

Following the fisherman was turning out to be more difficult than we had expected. The path on our side led away from the top of the river bank, leaving a wall of thick vines, thorny bushes, and poison ivy between us and the view.

"We can take a look from the Leaning Tree," Charlie said.

The Leaning Tree was a natural observation post. Robert had named it. It was a big white pine that slanted out over the river. Years ago a bad storm had torn half its roots out of the ground and pushed the tree over to a forty-five-degree angle. Now the top branches stuck way out over the rocks and rapids below. Robert used to climb up above the thick brush and all the way out to the end. Nobody else ever went that far. He said he could see for miles, up and down the river. He used to spend hours in the very highest branches, hanging way out above the rocks and water.

When we reached the tree, Milo sat down on a rock.

"Following this guy was your idea, Luke," he said. "Go on up and tell us what you see."

I took a long look at the tree's exposed roots. Then I stared up at the top hanging out over the riverbank. "I don't know, Milo," I said. "I'm not sure it would hold me." I knew I wasn't sounding like much of a leader, but the rocks and the river were an awful long way down. In my head I could hear Mom saying, "Be careful, Luke. Don't be foolish. Try to remember what happened to Robert."

Milo rolled up his eyes. "Yeah, right," he said. "You're so much heavier than Robert." He turned to his brother. "I guess it's up to you, Charlie. You're the lightest."

"Also the scaredest," Charlie replied. "There's no way I'm going up that thing."

Milo switched into his Captain Bligh voice: "And so it is that even my veddy own brutha has failed me," he said, placing his hand on his heart. "Were I still in command of this vessel, I'd have you both flogged." With a sigh, he reached for the lowest branch and began to pull himself up the tree. As he climbed he switched into a new role. "The forward observer takes his post in full view of the enemy lines," he said. There he goes again, I thought. I wondered if pretending to be somebody else helped keep Milo from being scared.

When he was about thirty feet off the ground, the tree gave a sudden loud groan. Dirt and sand trickled out from between its roots. I sucked in my breath.

"Come on down, Milo," I said. "It's too dangerous."

"You'll break your neck, Milo," Charlie shouted.

Milo paused long enough to look down at the base of the tree. It still seemed to have a good grip on the ground.

"False alarm," he said, starting upward again. He knocked loose a pine cone, and I listened to see how long it would take to land on the rocks below, but I couldn't hear it because the rapids were too loud.

"His car's gone!" Milo shouted when he reached the top of the tree. "Wait a minute. I see it moving along the road. He fell for it! He thinks he's putting one over on us. He's heading *upstream*."

Milo started to back slowly down the tree, a much trickier proposition than the climb up.

"We've got to watch what he does," Charlie said. "But he's got a car. He'll get there way before us."

"Not if we hurry," I said. "He can't do anything until he finds the farmer and rents a boat. If we run, we can be there before he gets on the river."

Charlie and I took off up the path.

"Thanks for waiting, guys," Milo called after us as he let go of the lowest branch and landed with a thump on the ground.

13. THE FORT

After nearly half an hour of crashing along the over-grown path, we came to an open meadow that ran along the water. This seemed like a whole different river from the one we knew. It was deep and the current was slow. The surface was like smooth black glass with barely a rock in sight. The stillness was the first thing that hit me. The rapids where we fished were too far away to be heard. Here, the caw of a crow was a big deal. We could actually hear the honey bees in the meadow flowers.

"I don't see any sign of him yet," Charlie whispered.

The high banks were missing along this section of the river. The land on both sides sloped gently to the water. On our side we could see an old mattress, some logs, and a bunch of boards and branches scattered in a line across the field—junk left behind by high water. Across the river we could see a dozen black and white Holsteins, grazing calmly in the pasture between the river and some run-down barns. If you looked up the river, you could see blue mountains in the distance.

Thunk!

It was the sound of wood on wood. It echoed back and forth across the smooth surface of the water. Next came a rattling sound. Somebody was fitting oars into a rowboat's oarlocks.

"Come on," I said, ducking down and pushing out through the waist-high grass. "We can hide in the Fort."

The three of us crept toward a collection of rocks in the middle of the meadow about thirty feet from the edge of the river. There was a wide flat rock in the center, sur-rounded by a half dozen smaller rocks. The rocks on the river side stood on end, so we could lie on the flat rock behind them and nobody could see us from the river. We called it the Fort. Sometimes we had used it to hold off Apaches. Other times it had protected us from the death rays of alien invaders.

Milo usually decided who we were and which partic-ular enemy we were fighting. He was the best at pre-tending. What the rest of us saw as a tree, Milo would see as the mast of a clipper ship. Even Robert, when he used to play with us, had to admit that Milo was good at it. He let Milo make all the stuff up, and Milo would always give him the best part. If Milo invented a ship, Robert would get to be captain. Then Milo'd declare himself the first mate and the rest of us would wind up as crew. After Robert died, Milo was always captain. We didn't really mind, but it wasn't the same.

When we reached the Fort, we each stretched out behind a rock. From our hiding places, we could hear the slow, rhythmic swooshing of water and the creak of the oarlocks as the fisherman rowed toward the center of the river. Suddenly, the sounds stopped. Charlie peeked out from behind his rock.

"The rat," he said. "He's baiting his hook with *our* bait."

"Well, Luke gave it to him," Milo said. Charlie gave me a scowl.

"He might just as well use a bare hook up here," I said. "He's not going to catch anything."

We watched as the boat drifted slowly downstream while the fisherman sat and fiddled with something in his hands.

"He probably doesn't even know that the point should go under the collar," Charlie said, still thinking about our hellgrammites. "And he'd better clip off the tail hooks. Or it'll snag him on the bottom. I hope it does."

"Too deep," Milo muttered.

"He'll need a sinker," I added.

Ker-splash! A loud smack on the water shattered the stillness.

"Holy smoke! What was that?" Charlie asked. We could see big rings on the surface of the water, starting about ten yards from the boat and spreading slowly toward both shores.

"Something jumped, and it had to be enormous," Milo said.

"I thought you said there were only carp and catfish up here," Charlie said. "Can catfish jump? If that was a smallmouth, it was a monster."

The fisherman almost fell out of the boat in his rush to get his line in the water. When he finally had out enough line, he sat down to wait. We watched as he drifted slowly in the still water until he was forty or fifty yards below us. Nothing happened, so he laid his pole in the stern of the boat and began to row upstream to repeat the process.

He was just about even with us again when we heard the high whine of his reel and the clatter of metal dragging across wood. We saw him lunge for his pole and raise the tip over his head until it was bent over like a McDonald's arch.

"Yee-hah!" the fisherman shouted. He sounded as if he were riding a steer in a rodeo.

We stood up to watch. We couldn't believe it. The fish was heading upstream. It had to be big because the boat wasn't drifting. The fish was stronger than the current. Twice the fish leaped and landed with an incredible splat, loud enough to frighten the cows.

The fisherman leaned over one side of the boat and plunged his net into the water. Spooked by the net, the fish took two more runs away from the boat, but he was tiring. The next time he approached the boat, the battle was over.

When the fisherman stood up, he saw the three of us watching from shore. He held the net up high so we could see what was in it. The fish was bent into a *U* with both the head and the tail sticking up out of the top of the net. The sun flashed on its silvery scales.

"A smallmouth," said Charlie.

"A *giant* smallmouth," Milo said. "Got to be at least sixteen inches."

I felt like crawling under one of the rocks. Boy, I sure put one over on that guy. No bass up here? What a dope I was. At least we wouldn't have to worry about him messing around our fishing holes anymore.

Then I noticed that Milo was staring at me. He had that same look on his face that he had when he was staring up at the hornets' nest with a rock in his hand. "Are you thinking what I'm thinking?" he asked. "If we're going to win the bet, we have to get ourselves out into the middle of this part of the river."

14·THE RAIN

The rain started that night while I was asleep. I'm not sure what woke me. My cot was all the way at the back of the screened-in porch, so no water blew in on me. Maybe it was the grumbling of the thunder in the mountains upriver that disturbed me. Or the way the flashes of lightning lit up the wall by my bed like a movie screen. It could have been the change in the sound of the rapids. That's what told me that the river was rising.

When the river is low, the rapids sound like a million tiny waterfalls. They make a happy, playful sound as the water tumbles over and around the stones on its way to smoother going downstream. But as the river rises and more and more of the rocks get hidden below the surface the noise becomes less complicated but somehow more threatening. It sounds deeper, more solid, more powerful. You can hear the river getting ready to push things out of its way.

Robert's cot used to be right next to the screen at the edge of the porch, between me and the rest of the world. Sometimes, when I wake up in the night, I miss him so much that I keep my eyes closed and pretend he's still there, propping his head on one hand and staring down at the river. I remember the nights when he'd realize that I was awake and he'd talk to me.

"You like to read, don't you, Luke?" he asked me once.

I didn't know what to say. I always felt guilty when I surfaced from deep in a favorite book and discovered that Robert was looking at me. "I guess so," I mumbled.

"You guess so?" He sighed. "I'd give my right arm to be able to read like you."

After Robert's accident, my dad asked me if I wanted to move my cot inside. I told him that I would rather stay out on the porch, even though it meant sleeping alone. I felt closer to Robert out there.

It was still raining—not hard but steady—when I stopped at Milo's cabin on my way to the beach. I was wearing a yellow plastic rain jacket over my bathing suit. Charlie was in the front yard, trying to keep a big black umbrella over his head while he struggled to work a backlash out of his reel.

"Where's Milo?" I asked.

"Got me," Charlie replied. "He was gone when I got up for breakfast. He's probably fishing already."

"He'd better be," I said. "There's only a week left, and I bet night crawlers taste pretty gross."

Charlie and I headed down to the beach. When we got there, there was no Milo in sight. In fact, there was only half a beach. The water must have risen at least a foot in the night. The shoreline had moved halfway up the sand. The mudhole path was on its way to becoming a canal. Hannah and Ursula were just upstream from the mudhole on a wide flat rock that was only three feet from shore.

"Catch anything?" I asked.

"Not recently," Ursula said, with the rain streaming down her face. "We just came out for the nice weather. Anyway, we've already caught the fish that's going to win the bet."

"That eleven-incher?" Charlie scoffed. "There's lots bigger bass than that in this river."

I was afraid that he was going to say more, but then he seemed to remember that Milo had threatened him with horrible tortures if he told the girls what the fisherman had caught up by the Fort.

"Where's Milo?" Hannah asked.

"We don't know," I answered.

"He's probably up to something," Ursula said. "Some-how I don't trust that guy."

"He feels the same way about you," Charlie said.

"I wouldn't try to make it out to the island," Hannah said. "Or what's left of it," she added.

I stared across at the pile of rocks that Charlie had populated with imaginary snakes. All of the small stones were out of sight already. The curling waves made the big rocks look like speedboats that were heading upstream. Between the island and shore the current was moving a lot faster than usual, and I figured that the water would be above my waist.

Charlie and I decided to forget about fishing from the island. We moved up the shore past the girls until we were about fifty feet above them. We stopped at a place where the land poked out in a stubby peninsula. Settling down on the end, we tossed out our lines and let them drift toward the girls. Almost immediately, the strong current swept our baits to the surface, so we reeled in and tied on some sinkers. Then we tried again.

This time it was only seconds before the tip of Charlie's rod dipped. "Got something," he said and started to reel in his line. "Feels pretty big," he said, but I knew he was pulling both the fish and the sinker against a sizeable current. When he finally lifted the fish out of the water, the girls whooped and hollered and danced on their rock. Charlie's catch was a baby sunfish, about four inches long.

"Hey, Charlie," Ursula shouted. "What's the matter? Did your fish shrink in the rain?"

15·THE NAILS

I had a pretty good idea what Milo was doing, but I wanted to make sure. I decided to get up early the next day and follow him when he left. I borrowed an alarm clock from my grandmother. It was a big round old-fashioned clock that stood on four small legs. There were two shiny bells on top with a sort of hammer between them. I figured that it must make an awful racket, but I didn't think that anybody would hear it from the porch.

"Your grandfather and I used to set this so that we could watch the sun come up over the river," Grandma said. She smiled at the memory and closed her eyes. Her lips moved, and I knew she was talking to Grandpa again. He'd died when I was two, but Grandma still talked to him every day. I wondered if talking to Robert might keep me from missing him so much.

I set the alarm clock for five A.M. I didn't think that Milo would be going anywhere before that. When I woke up, it was still dark. I rolled over and looked at the time. Almost seven o'clock! I'd slept through the alarm. What had happened to the sunrise? Then I heard thunder and realized that it was still raining. Actually, it was coming down in buckets. The darkness had nothing to do with the time.

I pulled on my damp bathing suit, grabbed my plastic rain jacket, and, being careful not to let the screen door slam, I crept down the steps at the end of the porch. The smell of frying bacon came out to meet me as I slipped past the kitchen. My mother spotted me through the kitchen window.

"Luke, don't you want some breakfast?" she asked, appearing in the doorway.

"No time, Mom," I said. "I'm meeting the guys."

"Well, you stay away from that river," she said. "It's getting higher by the minute."

My first stop was Milo's place. I was surprised to see that Charlie was out in the front yard, floating sticks down a little stream that had formed in a tire track. It was pretty early for Charlie to be up.

"Where's Milo, Charlie?" I asked.

"He's not here," Charlie answered, not looking up from his sticks.

"I figured that out. Did he say where he was going?"

"The Fort."

"That jerk," I said, moving off.

"I'm coming," said Charlie. "But we have to make sure that the girls don't follow us. Milo'd kill me."

Charlie and I made good time on the path. Somebody had cut down a lot of the saplings. It had to have been Milo. His uncle had given him a machete that was so sharp he could chop down an inch-thick tree with one whack.

"He kept talking about needing a boat," Charlie said. "But that was before the river got so high. There's no way he could get to the other side now." He paused for a moment. "Is there?" he asked.

"Not unless he's crazy," I said. It didn't make any sense. Even Milo wouldn't steal a boat. At least I didn't think he would.

As the sound of the rapids faded behind us, I started to hear another sound—a steady tapping. The nearer we got to the Fort, the louder the taps.

When we reached the meadow, we could see Milo bent over, surrounded by boards. His back was glistening in the rain, and he was swinging a hammer. I was surprised to see how close the shoreline had moved to the the Fort. The river had climbed over its banks and, because the ground was so flat, the water was spreading across the meadow. Milo looked up and saw us as we approached him across the field.

"The girls don't know," Charlie shouted. He wanted to make sure he wasn't in trouble before Milo could reach him.

"They'd better not," Milo said, scowling. Then he stood up and pointed proudly at the ragged row of boards that he had started to nail across two fence posts.

"This, gentlemen," he said, "is our secret weapon."

I couldn't believe he was serious. I looked from the rickety boards to the rising river. "You've got to be kidding," I said.

"Well, I'm not." Milo started to bang in another nail. The rain was coming down even harder. You could hear it sizzle on the surface of the water.

"You can't go out there on this thing, Milo," I said. "Not now. The river's getting dangerous."

"Maybe down at the rapids, but not up here. Look how smooth it is."

"It just *looks* the same. It's deeper and faster. And it's still rising. Another half hour and it will be up to the Fort."

"That's why we've got to hurry, Luke. We're running out of time. Pretty soon the river will be so muddy and full of washed-down junk that the fish won't be able to see our bait. The fishing will be shot for the rest of the week. We've got to get out there *now*."

"We?" I asked. "Did I hear 'we'? Forget that 'we' stuff, Milo. I'm not riding a flood on a pile of sticks. This thing looks like the second little pig's house after the wolf got through with it."

"You're not going? How come I'm not surprised?" Milo said. "How about you, darling brother?"

There was a flicker of lightning in the distance. Charlie stared at his feet. "It's too small for two people," he said. "I'd better wait here with Luke."

"You guys are something," Milo said, shaking his head. He banged the last nail home, laid down the hammer and straightened up, using his hands to push the cramp out of his back. His wet black hair was plastered across his forehead, and rain was running off his chin. "Come on, then," he said, putting his hands under one side of the raft. "At least you can help me move it to the water."

"You're crazy," I said, but I grabbed the fence post on my side. Charlie got in front with his back to the raft so he could lift up on the boards. The whole thing was heavier than it looked, but the three of us were able to handle it. We would have made it all the way to the water in one carry if Milo hadn't slipped in the mud when we were about ten feet from the edge.

Charlie and I tried to keep the raft level when Milo went down, but it twisted in our hands and the nails started to pop. We lowered it to the ground as quickly as possible, but not before about a third of the boards had come loose at one end.

"The nails are too short, Milo," I said.

"Or the boards are too thick," added Charlie, helpfully.

"It would have made it if I hadn't slipped," Milo said, leaning down to rinse the mud off his hands in the water. "I'll get the hammer."

"You're going to have to *tie* it together, Milo," I said. "These nails are like thumbtacks."

"I don't have enough rope. I used it all for the anchor line."

He pointed to a rock that was lying over near the Fort. It was shaped like a loaf of French bread. A piece of rope about ten feet long was tied around the middle.

"That won't even reach the bottom, Milo," I said. "Don't you get it? The river's *high* and it's getting *higher!*"

"Well, that's all I've got." Milo started to hammer the raft back together again. "And it's all I need. I'll use that pole to push me wherever I want to go."

A long thin stick lay on the ground near the water. It looked about twice as big around as a fishing rod.

"You call that thing a pole?" I asked. "It's too thin. And you can't push something that's falling apart." I was feeling frustrated and a little bit scared. Then I had an idea.

"Charlie, you round up some thinner boards," I said. "I'll run back to the cabin and get some rope to tie this thing together. And I'll make sure there's enough left over for a decent anchor line. Milo, just don't do anything until I get back."

Milo didn't say anything. He went on pounding the nails back into place.

"At least we won't have to lift it again," Charlie said. I saw what he meant. While we were arguing, the water had been spreading across the meadow. Now it was only three feet from the front of the raft.

16·MILO'S SECRET

I could only think of one rope that was long enough. And taking that rope was going to get me into *big* trouble. But I couldn't let anyone stop me, and I didn't have time to explain. Gasping for breath, I burst out of the woods and ran toward our cabin. I didn't see anybody around.

I crawled under the porch and dragged out an old wooden ladder. I carried it across the yard and leaned it up against our big maple tree. The tree was in the far corner of the property a long way from the house, right at the top of the river bank. Nothing went right. First, the top of the ladder slid sideways on the tree. Then the bottom slipped backwards in the wet grass. When I was reasonably sure that the ladder wasn't going to go over the bank and toboggan me into the river, I started to climb. When I looked up, the rain got in my eyes and made it hard to see where I was going. But it was a lot better than looking down. Finally, my feet reached the third rung from the top, and I was able to put one arm around the tree. I reached up with the other and grabbed the new clothesline that my father had put up less than three days ago. The end hadn't even been cut and a thick coil of extra line hung down next to the pulley wheel.

I stole a quick look at the house. If Mom saw me halfway up a wet tree at the edge of the river bank, she'd go into orbit. There was no sign of life in the house. I was lucky.

I slipped the pulley off its hook and let everything fall. Then I backed down to the ground and wound the line around my left arm, stretching the coils between my palm and my elbow. I knew that clothesline rope wasn't very strong, but at least I had a lot of it.

I never made it back to the Fort.

It was slow going right from the start. The rain had figured out a dozen different ways to ruin the path. Where the path had been mossy, the rain made it slippery. Where it had been dirt, the rain had turned it into mud. The low spots were now lakes. What was worse, I kept snagging the coil of rope on tree branches and saplings and getting brought up short like a lassoed calf.

When I was about halfway between our cabin and the

Fort, I heard footsteps crashing through the brush up ahead. They were accompanied by a sort of wheezing, moaning sound.

"He's *gone!*"

Charlie came charging out of the bushes. There was a frantic look in his eyes. His shirt was torn and his cheeks were wet with more than rain.

"He's gone!" he wailed. He stopped and bent over with his hands on his knees while he gasped for breath.

"Hold on. Get a grip, Charlie," I said, taking hold of his shoulders. "Tell me what happened."

"Everything . . . went . . . wrong," he said, sucking in breath between the words. His whole body shuddered. "He wouldn't . . . wait . . . until . . . you got back."

"Is Milo fishing on the river?"

"He's GONE!" A great sob forced its way up from his chest. Then the words came tumbling out, all in a rush. "He didn't even get to fish. He was just pushing off. The current sucked him out from shore. It spun him into the center. He threw over the anchor rock and nothing happened. He shoved that skinny pole down in front of the raft, and it snapped. He was speeding away from me. I couldn't do anything. It was raining so hard I couldn't see."

"But where is he now?"

"How do I know? He's GONE! Down the river. Heading for the rapids!"

I closed my eyes and took a big breath. "Okay,

Charlie. Take it easy," I said, trying to sound calmer than I felt. "Don't worry. He'll pass lots of stuff on the way. He'll probably just jump off the raft and swim to a rock or something. Or maybe even to shore."

"No, he won't," Charlie said and he started to cry.

"Why not?" I asked.

"Because Milo can't swim."

17 · THE ROOTS

I felt like a dope. All those years of Milo saying, "Swimming's a waste of time. Swimming's for juveniles. Swimming's for idiots." And it never, ever dawned on me. I'd thought it was just Milo being Milo. I tried to remember even one time that I had seen him swimming— between a couple of rocks, across a pool, or maybe right off the beach. Nothing. Not once. Not ever. I couldn't believe how blind I'd been.

"We'll never catch up to him. We've got to get help," Charlie said.

To do what? I wondered, but I kept my mouth shut. We were headed back down toward the cabin again, slipping and sliding along the path. I shifted the coil of rope to my other shoulder.

"We can't even see the river from here," Charlie said, staring at the thick tangle of sumac, poison ivy, and thorn bushes that formed a small jungle between the path and the water. "We don't know where he is or what's happening to him."

"We'll know in a minute," I said. "We're almost back to the Leaning Tree. We'll be able to see the whole river."

When we got there, the roots of the tree looked like shiny white bones in some tree-root graveyard. They were sticking way up out of a sea of brown mud. A lot of the dirt that had been around them had disappeared in the rain. A stiff breeze was twisting the top of the tree, but it was still hanging in there. It didn't look like the angle of the trunk had changed.

"It's practically out of the ground," Charlie said. "Look how much bank has washed away."

I didn't bother to answer. I just started to climb. And, as I climbed, a question crawled out of the back of my brain: Why now? it asked. Why can you do it now when you couldn't do it three days ago?

In close to the trunk, smooth wet branches circled the tree like a spiral staircase. Most of the growth was out at their ends. I felt like I was climbing inside a green tunnel that somebody had tipped up toward the sky.

When I stopped to catch my breath and looked down at the bottom of the tree, I saw another big chunk of dirt break loose from between two of the roots. It rolled down into the water and melted away. I started to climb again. I decided not to look down anymore.

"Can you see anything yet?" Charlie asked. I didn't waste my breath on an answer.

The first opening in the branches was on the downstream side of the tree. It was hard to see with all the rain coming down, but way off in the distance I could make out a crowd on the front lawn of our cabin. I thought that I saw Ursula and Hannah near the edge of the river bank. And somebody short—maybe my grandmother. I wondered if my parents were there. Everybody was standing in the rain but I didn't see any umbrellas. It looked like somebody was pointing up the river.

I pulled myself a couple of branches higher. Here the growth opened up in front of me and I could see the whole river. I couldn't believe it had gotten so high so fast. Most of the smaller rocks had disappeared already. But there were still plenty of really big ones sticking up out of the water, and quite a few others that were barely breaking the surface. And hung up on one of those last ones, about twenty-five yards upstream from the rapids, was what was left of the raft.

"I see it," I shouted. "It's stuck on a rock."

At first I didn't think there was anybody on it. Then there was a movement, and I could see Milo, lying flat across it, hanging on to one side. The current between Milo and our side of the river was awesome. I couldn't see a single rock above water between the raft and the shore, but a half dozen were still visible leading out into the river quite a ways upstream from the raft. I wondered . . .

Crack!

The roots! I must have gotten careless in all the excitement and moved around too much. One of the bigger roots was giving up, and the tree was coming down. I could feel myself falling. It was like being trapped in a green elevator. Worst of all, I knew that my part of the tree stuck out way beyond the edge of the bank.

I wrapped both arms around the trunk and did my best imitation of a grizzly bear. There was a loud snapping and crunching all around me as the falling tree broke off the branches of smaller trees and crashed down through the saplings and underbrush. In the midst of it all I heard a really blood-chilling sound. I guess I'd never heard Charlie scream before.

And then, suddenly, it was over. The tree didn't keep going. It didn't go tumbling down the bank. It stopped, stuck out level and straight like the flagpole on the side of a building. If I had been hanging down by both hands, I would have been the flag, snapping and blowing in the wind. But I'd managed to shinny around while it was falling so that now I was lying on top. I tried not to look down, but I couldn't help getting a glimpse of the foaming water straight below. At the far end of the tree I could see how many roots had pulled out and didn't want to think about how few were left in the ground.

I crawled along the tree trunk at caterpillar speed, trying to ignore its creaks and groans. My mouth was dry and I could feel my heart thumping away. The broken pine branches smelled like a living room on Christmas morning.

When I finally got to the end, I slid off and felt my feet squish into the not-so-solid ground. Charlie was big-eyed and wet and trembling all over, but none of the branches had got him. I didn't see any scratches or anything.

"Come on," I said, picking up the coil of rope. "We've got to go get Milo."

18·FIVE JUMPS

Ursula and Hannah met us at the edge of the river.
"Your father's coming," Ursula said.

"We can't wait," I gasped. "Here, Charlie. Can you tie
a bowline? Take this and tie it around a real solid tree."

Charlie took the end of the rope in his hands, but he
didn't move. He just stood there. "I'm not that great with
knots," he said finally. I wondered if it were true. I bet a
lot of people would think twice about trusting their knots
when their brother's life was at stake. I looked at Ursula
and Hannah.

"Give it to me. I'll do it," Ursula told Charlie. But
then she turned to me and said, "Luke, there's no way you
can swim that current."

"I'm not going to try," I said.

I started upstream along the shore, paying out the clothesline behind me. The bank was steep, and I had to limp along with one foot higher than the other. The usual shoreline had disappeared into the river. Rebel weeds swirled under the surface, turning the water into purple paint.

I tried to keep an eye on Milo. Once I almost stopped breathing when I saw the raft shift and spin almost completely around, but it stayed on the rock.

When I finally reached the string of rocks that led out from the shore, I took a quick look back at the girls. They had been joined by my father and Mr. Perkins. My father was shouting something, but I couldn't understand him over the noise of the water.

The first rock wasn't too far—maybe three feet from shore—and, lucky for me, it was pretty wide. I wondered how much the rope was going to hold me back. I'd have to guess at how much to uncoil before each leap. If the rope caught on something, I was going to stop in midair and drop into the river like a stone.

My father was coming up the shoreline toward me. I knew he would probably try to stop me, so I didn't have any time to waste. I uncoiled about five feet of rope and laid it carefully on the bank. I kept the rest on my shoulder. This was going to have to be a standing broad jump. There was no way to get a running start. I swung my arms out behind me, then swung them forward and launched myself into the air. I hadn't figured on the extra weight on one side from the rope. If the rock had been narrower, I would have fallen sideways into the river, but because there was room to step to the right, I caught my balance in time. I went into a crouch and looked at Milo.

He had raised himself to his knees and was holding his hands up, pushing his palms in my direction, signaling me to go back. I knew he didn't think I could make it. I also knew that I had to try.

The next two rocks were smaller, but because I had learned to lean to the left as I landed, I managed to keep my balance. There were still two big jumps to go. I knew I had to be careful to keep the rope behind me out of the water. If it got in the river, the dead weight would drag me in after it, or, at least, make it impossible to go on. I looked back and saw my father had reached the place where I had left the shore. He had the rope in his hand. He was holding it high so it wouldn't touch the water between the rocks. He just stared at me. He didn't say anything.

I turned around to check the water between me and the next jump. All kinds of strange things were floating by. I saw the top of a picnic table pass one end of a baby's crib. The next rock was high in front but low in the back. I'd have to clear the edge and then sit down fast to keep from tumbling downhill into the water. The rock also had a nasty crack with some weeds growing out of one side.

I uncoiled a handful of line, took a step backward, took a bigger step forward, and launched myself into the air. I cleared the leading edge all right, but I would have pitched forward down the slope if I hadn't managed to grab a handful of weeds. My feet slid out from under me and I went down hard on my back, but I hung on.

I was directly upstream from Milo now, but that wasn't good enough. Once I was in the water, I knew that the rope was going to start to swing me toward shore.

Which meant one more leap to go. And it was a killer. It reminded me of Ursula's jump from Shipwreck Rock. I'd have to land one foot on a small smooth rock that was barely breaking the surface, and then, without stopping, push off to a much bigger rock just beyond. There were about ten feet of rope left. I tied a loop in the end just in case I started speeding downstream sooner than I planned.

I pictured Ursula in my mind and took off, swinging my arms ahead of me. My right foot hit smack in the middle of the small wet rock, and my weight carried me forward to the bigger rock where I collapsed in a heap. Except for a scraped knee and a little blood running down my leg, everything turned out fine. I held up the end of the rope and pointed to it so that Milo could see the loop. He shook his head as if he thought I was out of my mind. The water must have risen some more because I couldn't see much rock showing under his raft.

I uncoiled the last bit of line, held it in one hand, and slipped the loop over my wrist. I stared down at the water. It was as brown as chocolate from all the dirt that was washing down off the banks. I was farther out from shore than Milo now, but I still wasn't sure it was far enough. I went to the edge of the rock and leaped as far as I could toward the other side of the river.

19. YOU'RE CRAZY!

I hit the water and went under. As I battled back to the surface I felt something dragging down my arms. Oh, no! I still had my rain jacket on. Dumb! Real dumb! But there was nothing I could do about it now. I had bigger problems.

I was moving too fast. I felt like a skier who had gotten caught in an avalanche. When my head came up out of the water, I could see that I had gone out one jump too far. I was heading straight downstream a mile a minute. The current was going to sweep me past the far side of Milo's rock. I tried to pull myself toward shore with one arm, but it wasn't working. Then I felt a tug on my wrist. The rope was taking hold. It was tightening between me and the tree on the shore. And it was starting to pull me toward Milo. I picked up even more speed.

I went under again. When I surfaced I saw that I had another worry. Milo, his raft, and his rock were all coming at me like a freight train. I knew that I was the one who was moving, but that's how it looked. I was going to arrive with a *splat*. I'd never be able to hang on. I swung my feet around so that they would be downstream ahead of me to cushion the blow. But it never came.

I missed. I came in low and outside like a bad curve ball, passed Milo's rock from about two feet away, and then swung up behind it when my rope caught across the front. I felt my feet touch another rock just under the water and I braced my heels against it. I had arrived.

"Luke, you're crazy!" Milo said, twisting around toward me. To tell you the truth I wasn't feeling totally sane.

"Just tie this fast," I said, holding on to the raft with one hand and working the loop off my wrist. A couple of the boards in the middle of the raft were missing, so there was a space where he could snake the line around one of the fence posts.

Milo threw a couple of half hitches around the post and then added another for good measure. "It won't work," he said with his teeth chattering. "It'll pull apart."

"Well, you can't stay here," I said. "The river is still rising. In five minutes you'll be down in those rapids. Then it'll really break up."

Using the big rock to shield me against the force of the water, I paddled around behind it until I could reach the edge of the raft on the other side. "You're going to lie flat," I said. "And you're going to hang onto the side where the rope is tied. I'll hold on here at the end of these boards. And the rope will swing us in to shore."

"Luke. You know I can't . . ." He gulped and stared at the rushing water.

"I know you can't swim," I said. "You're not going to have to."

"But there are a million rocks just under the water between here and the shore. You'll get bashed to pieces. Or the rope will hang up and leave us dragging under the water out here."

"No, it won't!" I was shouting at him even though we were only a couple of feet apart. I wanted to believe what I was saying. "It'll be just like when you cast across a current," I said. "The line tightens up and stays on top of the water. That's why you need a sinker."

"Maybe you're the sinker."

"I hope not," I said. "Are you ready?"

He didn't get a chance to answer. Suddenly, the raft tipped and slid off the rock. Here we go, I thought, tightening my grip. Milo was flat on his stomach hanging onto the upstream edge. I was clinging to the ends of the boards on one side. And it was working just like I'd planned. We were zooming down the river like an express train in a big arc that would take us in to shore about twenty yards below the tree. The force of the water on the raft was keeping the rope tight and on the surface. My father's clothesline was finally getting its test. Unfortunately, the closer we got to shore, the bigger the strain on the line. Will it hold? I wondered. Or will it snap and send us spinning downstream into the rapids?

We were half lucky. The clothesline held. But the raft didn't. I could feel the nails starting to go. The boards in my grip were pulling loose from the fence post. Whenever one started to come loose, I'd switch to a new one, but I was rapidly running out of boards. At least Milo's going to make it, I thought. But I'm not. Then I felt something tightening around my neck. And I realized that Milo was holding onto me. By the collar of my rain jacket.

When we finally thumped into the shore, it felt like a million hands grabbed me and dragged me up the bank. I ended upside down, on my back, with my father's face right above mine.

"Pretty dumb, huh?" I said, knowing how much I must have scared him.

He looked kind of pale, but he managed a smile. "Pretty brave," he said.

"It sure was." I recognized Ursula's voice. "Luke's not afraid of anything."

20·THE FISH

Six days later I was standing alone on the beach in the late afternoon. It was hard to believe that this was the same river. The sun had been out for days, and the water had nearly dropped back to normal. Dragonflies darted in and out of the rebel weeds. A couple of hawks circled lazily overhead. Only a tire and a lawn chair hung up in the bushes about halfway up the riverbank showed how high the water had been just a few days ago.

I flipped open the bail on my spinning reel and cast upstream and across the current. My last hellgrammite. My last day on the river until next summer. We were all leaving tomorrow. Monday was Labor Day. On Tuesday, Milo, Ursula, and I would be starting sixth grade. I wondered if Ursula was scared. Sometimes she seemed more at home on the river than she did in school.

I watched the line begin to sink as it drifted toward me and circled back into the still water just above the beach. The whole place was too quiet. I kept hearing my parents talking to each other in my head. I heard them over and over, the same as I had heard them late that night after all the excitement. I had been lying on my cot on the porch, trying to calm down enough to go to sleep. But the window was open, and I could hear them talking in low voices in the living room.

"He can't spend his whole life trying not to be Robert," my father had said.

"But I remember what happened, and I get so frightened."

"Robert took chances that weren't necessary. Luke is different."

"He took a terrible risk today. It was foolish."

"It wasn't foolish." There was a long pause and I imagined my father staring at the backs of his hands until he got the words right that he wanted to say. "Taking chances to show off is foolish. Taking a chance to save a friend's life is *not*. It's brave. Luke is very brave, but he also knows how to be careful. And *you* have to learn to trust him."

I had held my breath while I waited for my mother's reply. "I know you're right," she said, finally. "And I don't want to change him. But you'll have to help me." She was speaking so softly that I could hardly hear her. "Luke is brave," she said. "I'm the one who's afraid."

A noise in the bushes behind me snapped me back to the present. It took me a second to figure out where I was. Then I realized that I wasn't lying on my cot on the porch anymore. I was standing on the beach with the tip of my rod bent over and pointing at the water as my line sizzled across the surface toward the deepest part of the pool.

What could be better? I thought. The last fish. On the last day. I planned to take my time with it. Then I realized that I couldn't have brought it in any faster if I'd wanted to. It was too powerful. The pole was throbbing. I eased off the drag to protect the line. Too strong for a smallmouth, I thought. Maybe I've hooked into an eel. Then it leaped.

A flash of silver! I couldn't believe my eyes! The biggest smallmouth I'd ever had on my line! And on the last day of summer vacation! I played him carefully back and forth across the pool, hoping and praying the line wouldn't snag on a rock. When he finally tired, I slid him up on the sand. He sparkled and shimmered in what remained of the sunlight. I wet my hands, picked him up tenderly, and held him against the markings on my pole. Just a trace over fifteen inches!

He tried to wriggle out of my hands, and I felt his power. He was just barely hooked through one lip. I eased the hook out, being careful not to do any damage. After wading out from the beach, I reached down and moved him gently back and forth in the water. Then I opened my hands.

At first he just floated, starting to turn on his side. Then with a sudden twitch of his tail he was gone, barreling out toward the swift current, heading down, down, down toward the bottom.

"See you next summer," I said. "You still have an inch to grow."

21·THE GIFT

Maybe they'll forget," Charlie said.

Milo shook his head. "Ursula never forgets anything."

"Well, they wouldn't make us do it now, would they? After all that's happened?"

"Only time will tell," I said.

It was the last night of vacation, so we were having a cookout. Dad had come home early, bringing hot dogs and hamburgers. He was helping Mom husk the corn. Charlie and Milo and I were building the fire.

"Uh-oh. Here they come," Milo said.

"Do you see what I see?" Charlie whispered.

Hannah had a book in her hand as usual. But Ursula was carrying a blue coffee can.

"This is for you, Milo," she said.

Milo took the can carefully as if it were filled with explosives. Charlie looked around for a place to hide.

"Go ahead. Open it, Milo. You've certainly earned it," Hannah said.

Slowly, Milo pried the plastic lid off the can. I watched his face. I expected some awful expression when he looked down at the slimy worms. Instead, he wrinkled his forehead. He reached into the can and took out a neatly folded piece of paper.

"Go ahead. Read it," Ursula said as we all gathered around. Hannah was smiling.

Milo unfolded the paper. It looked like a handmade gift certificate. The colored letters were big enough so that we could all read them in the firelight.

GOOD FOR 10 FREE SWIMMING LESSONS
AT THE SCHOOL POOL
Ursula & Hannah

Milo squeezed his eyes shut and made a face. Then he opened them again and grinned. Ursula and Hannah and I applauded. But the loudest sound of all was Charlie's sigh of relief.

Later, Ursula said something else, but only to me. "You won anyway, Luke," she said softly. "I watched you let the winner go." She paused, and then added, "Did you do it to keep me from having green hair?"

I was glad it was dark because I felt my face turning red, and it wasn't caused by the fire. "Are you out of your mind?" I sputtered, sounding as shocked as possible. "I just hate to clean fish!"

We were both cracking up when Milo came swaggering back into the firelight. He still had his gift certificate clutched in one hand, but his head was bent forward, and he was moving his arms like an Olympic swimmer.

"After greasing his entire body," Milo said in his most serious TV anchorman's voice, "the daring swimmer enters the Channel at Dover with nineteen miles of choppy seas between him and the coast of France."

"There he goes again," Ursula said. "Milo's back to abnormal."